The TINDIMS of Rubbish Island and the SPOOKY SECRET

Mother-daughter duo, Sally Gardner and Lydia Corry are keen conservationists. Sally is a Costa and Carnegie-winning author and Lydia's *Eight Princesses and a Magic Mirror* was a *Guardian* Book of the Year 2019. *The Spooky Secret* is the fifth book in this series following *The Tindims of Rubbish Island*, *The Tindims and the Turtle Tangle*, *The Tindims and the Ten Green Bottles* and *The Tindims and the Floating Moon*.

The TINDIMS of Rubbish Island

and the Spooky Secret

Sally Gardner & Lydia Corry

ZEPHYR

an imprint of Head of Zeus

9 7 5 3 1 2 4 6 8

A catalogue record for this book is available from the British
Library.

ISBN (PB): 9781804549285
ISBN (E): 9781804549292

Printed and bound in Great Britain by
CPI Group (UK) Ltd, Croydon CR0 4YY

MIX
Paper | Supporting
responsible forestry
FSC® C171272
FSC
www.fsc.org

Typesetting & design by Jessie Price

Head of Zeus Ltd
First Floor East
5–8 Hardwick Street
London EC1R 4RG

www.headofzeus.com

With all our love
to every Little
Long Legs who is a
conservationist.

SG and LC

hello!

Chapter One

In which we find out the Tindims don't do Halloween.

The Tindims don't do Halloween. They don't know what Halloween is. Tiddledim the explorer, who had written a book all about the Long Legs, had never said anything about dressing up as ghosts or witches. By Long Legs he means grown-ups and by Little Long Legs he means you.

The Tindims were busy that driftsea,

2

which is what
they call
autumn, a time
of mists and
fogs. There was
always so much
to do.

Along with the
harvest, pumpkins
had to be brought
in. Every year the Tindims hoped they
would grow bigger than they had the
year before. They never did. This was a
disappointment as one of their favourite
treats was pumpkin pie.

But they didn't mind too much,
because at this time of year strange and
wonderful things would often wash up in
Turtle Bay. After all, the Tindims' motto
is: 'Rubbish today is treasure tomorrow.'

And there
were jumpers
and scarves
to be knitted,
socks to be
mended. Oh — and
making Roo-Roo jam
and bottling fruits and pickles. Then it
was on to collecting wood so they could
keep warm when the days grew colder
and the nights grew longer. That's when
the Tindims like to sit around the fire,
toasting their tootsies and listening to a
good story. And
because they
didn't know
about
Halloween
there was
no need to

dress up and look spooky or go knocking on each other's doors, shouting, 'Trick or treat?' But this driftsea things were different and it all started with the small pumpkins.

Chapter Two

Where we meet Broom
the gardener who is
worried about strange
noises coming from the
pumpkin patch.

*B*room the gardener lived in a tall greenhouse. Driftsea was even busier for him than the other Tindims. There was so much to be harvested and carefully stored away. He liked everything to be neat and tidy for when wintery brightsea weather arrived. He collected all the wood and sticks he found and stacked them neatly in the wood shed, ready for when it grew cold.

That sunny floodtide – which is afternoon to us Long Legs and Little Long

Legs — Broom was in his garden with his wheelbarrow looking at the pumpkins. They were a sorry sight. *What is wrong with them?* he wondered. *They never grow big. This year there's hardly enough for one pumpkin pie.*

Broom yawned. He hadn't been sleeping well which wasn't like him. He wasn't sure if he was imagining things, but he was as sure as he was not sure that something or someone was following him. He even thought he'd heard it go, 'Boo'. But whoever this something or someone was they were invisible, for search as he might he couldn't see them.

Then he heard something or someone say, 'Those are the smallest pumpkins I've ever seen.'

Broom looked down and was surprised when sparks came from the pumpkins.

'Well, I never,' he said.

He took off his hat and put his ear to the ground, hoping to hear what was going on. He nearly jumped out of his green fur when Pinch, Skittle's furry purry pet, raced up to him.

'What are you doing?' Pinch asked.

'Oh...
nothing,'
said Broom,
blushing
and putting
his hat
back on. 'Just
wondering why the
pumpkins are so small again this year.'

'They are on the little side of nothing,'
said Pinch. 'I don't think they'll even
make good lanterns for Ethel B Dina's
café.'

Just then Pinch heard something
or someone say, 'That should do
the trick.'

'Who said that?' said Pinch.
'Oh, good,' said Broom.
'You can hear it too. What
a relief.'

'You mean,' said Pinch, 'you can hear someone talking who isn't me and isn't you?' He sniffed about, but the something or someone was nowhere to be found.

'It's very strange,' said Broom. 'And a bit spooky.'

'You can say that again,' said Pinch.

Chapter Three

In which Broom and Pinch decide help is most definitely needed. And we find out about Ethel B Dina's café.

'It's very strange and a bit spooky,' said Broom.

'Yes,' said Pinch. 'And saying it twice does make it sound a bit less spooky.'

They laughed until their tummies jelly-jiggled which made them feel a lot better.

As Skittle's mum, Admiral Bonnet, always said, 'If you can't laugh at something that worries you, the worry only gets bigger'.

'We should go and speak to Jug,' said Pinch. 'He's a fountain of facts.'

'The same idea is running round my hat band,' said Broom. 'Jug might find it funny and, more importantly, he might know what the something or someone is.'

'And that's a fact,' said Pinch as they set off to Ethel B Dina's café.

Ethel B Dina lived in a flat beneath Rubbish Island where she could see fishes swimming past her window. She ran the Fish Hospital and recently she'd felt it would be good for a few of her patients to stretch a fin, waggle a tail and have a different view of life.

She had asked Spokes and Barnacle Bow to build her an outdoor café with a wall of fish tanks so her patients could admire the wonders of Rubbish Island.

Ethel B Dina ran the café with Granny Gull. It was a great success and not only with the fishes. The Tindims met there for a good old natter especially at gleetime, which they always do properly with white table cloths, china teacups and plates, and a pot of Granny Gull's glee, which is tea to you and me.

Broom and Pinch walked together through the Roo-Roo Woods and as they walked they tried to think what the something or someone might be. Broom said he'd made up a poem in the middle of the

night, when he had been woken again by the something or someone huffing.

'It isn't finished,' he said, 'because I can't finish it without knowing what the something or someone is. So it's missing the last verse.'

'That's all right,' said
Pinch. 'I'm all ears.'
   They both found this
funny because Pinch did
have mighty furry purry ears.
   'I've called my poem
The Something or Someone,'
said Broom.

'Someone speaks when
            I'm not talking,

Something mumbles when I
            go away,

Someone follows me out walking,
Something's in the pumpkins today.

Someone, I tell myself, is nothing.

Something is decidedly not right.

Someone keeps me awake by huffing.

            Something spooks me out
            at night by huffing.

19

Chapter
Four

In which Jug wonders
what a witch is and
something happens at
the pumpkin patch.

*J*ug was enjoying a cup of glee at the café and reading from the latest washed-up and dried-out newspaper. There was an article on how to make a witch's costume and he was wondering what a witch was.

'Hello,' said Jug when he saw Broom and Pinch come out of the Roo-Roo Woods.

'Where are Skittle and Brew?' asked Pinch.

'Didn't you see them?' said Jug. 'They went to find you.'

'Oh,' said Pinch. 'But we are here.'

'I suppose
we weren't
here when they
went looking
for us,' said
Broom. He sat
down on a chair and
Pinch sat on another.
Broom began to tell Jug about the
something or someone and was making
quite a muddle of it. Pinch suggested it
might help if he recited his poem again.

*Someone speaks when I'm not talking,
Something mumbles when I—*

But before he could say another word
Skittle and Brew came bursting out of
the woods.

'You must come,' gasped Skittle.

'Now,' said Brew.

'What's happened?' asked Jug, who was Brew's dad.

'You have to see this,' said Skittle, taking a deep breath.

'Admiral Bonnet and Captain Spoons say they've never seen anything like it,' said Brew.

'Never seen what?' asked Ethel B Dina, bringing out a tray of freshly baked rock cakes.

'Just drop everything and come,' said Brew.

'Don't drop the rock cakes,' said Broom, taking one.

'Come where, my
still and sparkling darlings?'
asked Ethel B Dina.

Granny Gull came out of the kitchen.
'What's going on?'

'You must come and see what's
happened,' said Skittle.

Ethel B Dina put a 'Closed' sign
on the door of the café and told the
turtle in the turtle tank that he was in
charge. Then the little party of Tindims

ran through the Roo-Roo Woods to find
everyone else in Broom's garden. They
were looking at something but what they
were looking at only Broom could see
because he was the tallest Tindim.

'Well, I never,' he said.

'There you all are,' said Captain
Spoons. 'I saw them from my window and
couldn't believe my eyes. Catch me a
kipper. This must be the **BIGGEST**
pumpkin ever.'

'That's strange,' said Broom, 'because only this floodtide it was the smallest pumpkin ever.'

'And that's a fact, actually,' said Pinch.

Broom took off his hat and scratched his head. 'I've never known anything to grow as fast as these pumpkins.'

'This year we'll have a huge pumpkin pie,' said Granny Gull.

Broom shook his head. 'Something's not right,' he said.

Chapter Five

Where Broom has a fright
in the night and is sure
as sure can be that
the pumpkins are up to
something.

That ebbtide, which is evening to you and me, Broom tried to remember where he had found the pumpkin seeds. Then he remembered they'd been in a barrel that had washed up in Turtle Bay. That's how he knew they were called pumpkins. Jug had read the label. He thought they were supposed to grow quite big, at least they did for the Long Legs.

Broom called Jug on the phone and asked him to look again at the words on the back of the packet in case they'd missed something.

'It says they're perfect for Halloween,' said Jug.

'What's that?' asked Broom.

'Squeeze me a teabag, I don't know,' said Jug.

At moontide, which is midnight and very late, Broom sat in his greenhouse, thinking. From his armchair he had a good view of the largest pumpkin. He could hear huffing noises coming from it.

Broom worried a lot about his plants. But he'd never been frightened by a pumpkin before. And what was Halloween? Perhaps it was a secret ingredient, necessary to grow pumpkins.

He thought and thought until his
head hurt and he thought it was no
good sitting there feeling spooked. He
was not going to let a pumpkin get the
better of him. No, he was not. He pulled
himself out of his armchair, put on his
hat, wrapped his scarf round his neck
and opened the door. Taking a lantern he
went out to the pumpkin patch. And then
he stopped. They were even bigger. That
hadn't given him a fright. What scared
him was the sight of a pair of shiny red

shoes, running along by themselves, without legs, a body or a head.

The shoes were saying, over and over again, 'That's better, much better.'

Broom was so frightened he fell over a garden rake as he ran back to his greenhouse. He closed the door and locked it.

When neeptide arrived, he didn't even bother to look at the pumpkins, he went straight through the woods to Ethel B Dina's café.

'My dear still and sparkling darling,' she said, 'your fur has gone frizzy.'

'Last night I saw
a small pair of
red shoes
running all by
themselves,'
said Broom.

'How thrilling. Is
this to do with those pesky
pumpkins?' asked Ethel B Dina.

'Yes,' said Broom. 'And pesky they
are.' He stopped. 'What does "pesky"
mean?'

'Pesky...' said Ethel B Dina, looking
far out to sea, which meant she hadn't
a clue. 'I think, my still and sparkling
darling, we must go to find Jug and ask if

he has ever heard of a pair of red shoes walking and talking all by themselves.'

Mug and Jug, Brew and Baby Cup lived in a bungalow called All-Sorts because it had been made out of all sorts of things fished from the sea. When Ethel B Dina and Broom arrived, they were eating pancakes.

Broom did his best to explain, but when he got to the part about the small red shoes talking, Jug asked if this was a riddle from a cracker.

'No, it's what Broom saw last night near the pumpkins,' said Ethel B Dina.

'A small pair of red shoes walking and talking by themselves? Are you sure, Broom?' asked Jug.

Broom was a shy Tindim and everyone was looking so worried he nearly said he might have dreamed the red shoes. But he knew it was important to tell the truth.

'Well... yes. I'm as sure as sure can be they were small red shoes,' said Broom. Hoping to change the subject, but not by too much, he asked, 'What does "pesky" mean? Because it goes well with pumpkins.'

'It means troublesome,' said Jug.

'That's what the something or someone is,' said Broom.

'Whatever the something or someone is,' said Ethel B Dina, 'they shouldn't be here.'

They agreed it was a mystery. A mystery that made Rubbish Island seem full of shadows, which had never happened before.

Chapter
Six

In which Broom goes out
in the dark to look at
the pumpkins. And calls
for help.

nother day passed. On Monkday,
Broom checked on the pumpkins.
A weeping sound was coming
from the biggest. He couldn't tell if it
was the pumpkin weeping, or something
or someone inside the pumpkin. He bent
down to see better. What he saw was a
hole at the bottom of the pumpkin and
it looked as if the inside of the pumpkin
had been scooped out. He looked closer
and saw a little bed. It was made out of
one of his useful boxes, with a sock for a
mattress and a piece
of Granny Gull's
knitting for
a cover.

Strange, thought Broom. *Very strange.*
Then the whole pumpkin began to shiver
and shake. Broom jumped to his feet in
fright.

Quickly, he called Admiral Bonnet who
came with Captain Spoons to have a look
at the pumpkin for themselves.

They agreed that Broom should keep
an eye on it. All day he sat in his garden
watching the pumpkins. At ebbtide, he
was pleased to report to Captain Spoons
that they hadn't grown any bigger. And
nothing had come out of the big pumpkin.

'Good,' said Captain Spoons. 'And good
ebbtide to you.'

Which is goodnight to us Long Legs and
Little Long Legs.

Broom had washed up his supper plate
and put on his pyjamas when something
outside lit up and that something was the
pumpkins. Something or someone was out
there!

Broom took a mop and a trowel
and opened his door. Bravely, he
tiptoed on his furry toes to the
pumpkin patch.

To his surprise, they had all had scary faces carved into them and each face was lit up. If that wasn't bad enough, every pumpkin had been hollowed out. Broom could see that something or someone was hiding inside the largest pumpkin.

'Hello,' said Broom, his voice shaky.

HELP!

Something a bit like a jellyfish floated out of the pumpkin's eyes and back through its mouth. Broom felt his fur stand on end. Then a pair of stripy legs ran past him. It was too much. Broom couldn't deal with this by himself.

'HELP!' he cried as loudly as he could.

Chapter Seven

Where Captain Spoons
does something that
hasn't been done before.
This is an emergency.

*A*dmiral Bonnet was fast asleep, as were the other Tindims, all except Captain Spoons who was on moontide duty. The Tindims took it in turns to keep watch at moontide so Rubbish Island floated in calm waters and didn't bump into things like ships.

'Trumpets and tin hats! What's that?' said Captain Spoons when he heard Broom's call for help.

There was only one thing to do in an emergency like this, and that was to pull the emergency cord.

A bell rang in the engine room. It rang in All-Sorts bungalow. It rang in Ethel B Dina's underwater flat,

it rang at Barnacle Bow's and Granny Gull's houseboat, it woke Hitch Stitch, who lived at Turtle Bay. In a trice the Tindims were wide awake and getting ready to meet at Admiral Bonnet's house.

'What has happened?' they said. 'What shall we do?'

'Has anyone seen Broom?' Captain Spoons asked. 'I rang the emergency bell because I heard Broom call for help.'

At that moment a frightened Broom appeared.

'Oh, Broom,' said the Tindims. 'Are you all right?'

'No,' said Broom. 'I'm not. The something wafted and the someone has legs and no body and the pumpkins have faces.'

After much talk it was decided they would all go together to see what was happening. All, except of course for Baby Cup, who was fast asleep and stayed at Admiral Bonnet's house with Granny Gull.

The Tindims set off for Broom's greenhouse. Hitch Stitch was in front holding her hook for fishing bottles out of the sea, which she thought might come in handy. When they saw the pumpkins they couldn't believe they'd been hollowed out and the goodness in them had gone. But *where* had it gone?

'These are questions without answers,' said Broom. 'Where has the goodness gone? Why has it gone? And what is the point of scary pumpkin faces?'

Ethel B Dina said sadly, 'There'll be no pumpkin pies for us.'

Chapter Eight

In which Captain Spoons gives an order and everyone agrees that something must be done.

'No, no,' said Captain Spoons on Tunaday. 'No one is going out and that is an order.'

He had just finished talking to Hitch Stich. 'We don't know what the pesky pumpkins will do next,' he said to Admiral Bonnet.

'It's a good thing we have phones,' said Admiral Bonnet, 'otherwise how would we be able to stay in touch?'

'What's going on?' asked Skittle, coming up from her bedroom, yawning.

'Nothing's going on,' said Admiral Bonnet. 'But the nothing needs sorting out, so today will be an indoor kind of day.'

The phone rang again.
'Captain Spoons speaking,' said Captain Spoons. 'Trumpets and tin hats! Yes. No. That is strange. How many? And not cooked?' He hung up.

'What's going on?' asked Brew, sleepily climbing the stairs.

'What's going on?' asked Pinch, trotting up behind him.

'Ethel B Dina called to say there are about twenty unbaked pumpkin pies outside the houseboat. And she saw a little pair of hands putting a huge bag of pumpkin seeds outside her door.'

'Whose hands?' asked
Skittle.

'That's what we must
find out.'

'They must belong to
something or someone,'
said Pinch. *And that's
a fact.*

'But what or who? And
how did they get to Rubbish
Island?' asked Brew.

There were so many
questions looking for
answers.

'Where's Broom?'
asked Skittle.

'At home,
keeping watch,'
said Admiral
Bonnet.

'Shouldn't someone be with him?' said Skittle.

Captain Spoons phoned Broom to ask if he was all right. Broom didn't answer.

'Oh dear,' said Captain Spoons. He went outside and called, 'Broom, can you hear me?'

Still there was no reply. He tried the phone again.

'Yes,' said Broom. 'I didn't reach the phone in time. I was about to shout that nothing else has happened to the pumpkins.'

'The whole thing is odd,' said Admiral Bonnet. 'The trouble is, it's keeping us from recycling.'

Which was true. Usually the Tindims would be doing what they always do — fishing plastic bottles out of the sea and making useful things and treasures from the rubbish they found on the beach.

Captain Spoons
said he had spoken
to Spokes who had
spoken to Jug who had
suggested they call
Tiddledim the explorer
to ask if he knew what
the little hands, legs
and red shoes could
possibly mean and why
the pumpkins had scary
faces. And WHAT,
could anyone tell
them, is HALLOWEEN,
or for that matter, a
WITCH?

But Tiddledim the
explorer didn't answer.

Chapter Nine

In which Spokes invites a spooky guest to glee.

S pokes had been making
an extra-special surprise
for Brew and Skittle. He felt
the dark nights needed to be brightened
and he had come up with an interesting
invention, but it was missing an important
piece. Spokes had been waiting from
the last floodtide to the next floodtide
and still the important piece hadn't
washed up. He was keen to see what
the neeptide had brought in. But what
he wanted wasn't there and he walked
back along the shore to his home.
He lived above the engine room at
the foot of the island. His house
was a treasure trove of the
oddest bits and pieces
pulled from the sea.

Spokes put on the kettle and was
singing a Tindimish song:

'All I need is one piece more
But I can't find it on the shore.
It didn't turn up at low tide
And nothing useful did
I spy,'

when someone, who wasn't **Spokes**, sang:

'I could help with your discovery
Then the machine will be super lov-erly'

Hold on a minute, thought **Spokes**. That
wasn't me singing.

57

'Who's there? Show yourself,' said Spokes boldly.

'It's me, the School Ghost,' came the reply.

Floating before Spokes was a strange, white thing, like a jellyfish but with hands and arms. Spokes was not to be spooked. But as he didn't know what it was, he thought it best to ask.

'What are you?' he said. 'And where did you come from?' He felt a bit jelly wobbly, but refused to let the School Ghost get the better of him.

'Yippee!' said the School Ghost.
'You didn't run away like everyone else.'

'No,' said Spokes, standing firm.
'Do you have a name?'

'I did, but I've forgotten it.'

'I see,' said Spokes, who didn't see
at all.

'I'm the School Ghost. I have started
to fade because no one notices me
and I'm almost invisible.

Once I was a handsome ghost but now
I only have my hands and arms. My legs
went long, long ago.'

'That is sad,' said Spokes. He was
wondering about calling Captain Spoons,
then he thought he'd ask a few more
questions. Such as, was the School Ghost
on his own or were there more of him
floating around?

It was then the clock struck four:
gleetime. Which, as you know, is teatime
to Long Legs and Little Long Legs. It's
the most important time of a Tindim's
day and Spokes was not to be put off by
a school ghost. Out came a tablecloth,
napkins, a china gleepot, cups and saucers
and teaspoons, sandwiches with Roo-Roo
jam and Granny Gull's favourite muflops
and cake. Spokes laid two places.

Outside it started to rain, inside it was

warm and cosy by the fire. By the time
glee was over Spokes had forgotten the
questions he wanted to ask. So he
didn't find out that the School
Ghost hadn't come alone
to Rubbish Island.

Chapter Ten

In which Broom
invites a wet guest
to glee.

Rain pitter-pattered on Broom's greenhouse. The windows were so steamed up that he couldn't see out. He lit the fire and laid out the glee things. He had been looking forward to sitting down and had just poured his first cup of glee when there was a knock on the door. He opened it carefully because he didn't want the something or someone to come in, but he could see nothing.

'Hello,' said nothing. 'I'm rather hungry and wet. May I please come in?'

Broom closed the door quickly, for how can you let nothing into your home?

He'd tied his napkin round his neck and eaten the first of his Roo-Roo jam sandwiches when there was another knock on the door. *Perhaps*, thought Broom, *it's Ethel B Dina with a pumpkin pie*. He opened the door and again could see nothing.

'Hello,' said the same voice that had said hello the first time. 'I'm a someone, not a something, and I've been trying to be helpful but it's gone wrong.'

Still Broom could see nothing. But he could hear the someone's teeth chattering. He scratched the top of his

furry head and thought for a moment. He shivered. It was cold outside.

'If I can see nothing,' he said, 'how do I know you are a someone?'

To his surprise he felt something brush past him, leaving little muddy footprints on the floor behind them.

'Oh,' said the someone, 'you have such a lovely home.'

Broom, being a polite Tindim, said, 'Shall I take your coat and hang it up to dry?'

He felt a bit silly saying this as he couldn't see who he was talking to, or if they even had a coat.

'Thank you,' said the someone and handed Broom nothing, or nothing Broom could see, but it felt wet.

Broom hung it up and that's when he saw who the someone was. A young Long Legs girl. She wore a pointed hat, a green dress, blue striped stockings and small red shoes. She was tiny.

'What's your name?' asked Broom.

'Tilly Topple,' she replied. 'Oh — you can see me!' She sounded worried. 'Of course you can — you took my invisible cloak.'

'I didn't take it,' said Broom. 'You handed it to me.'

'So I did. I tore it and it has holes.'

Broom looked at his glee getting colder by the second and brought out another plate and cup and saucer and laid a place for Ms Tilly Topple.

'Thank you,' she said as she sat down to eat.

When she'd finished, she climbed into Broom's armchair by the fire and fell fast asleep. Broom had never had anyone stay at his greenhouse and once he had cleared away the dishes and swept the floor, he decided it was a nice feeling having another person there. He covered Tilly Topple with a hand knitted

blanket to keep her cosy. *Come neeptide,* he thought, *I have some important questions to ask her.* He wrote a list so he wouldn't forget.

QUESTION ONE
Where do you come from?
QUESTION TWO
Is there anyone with you?
QUESTION THREE
How did you get here?

He underlined the last question. Twice.

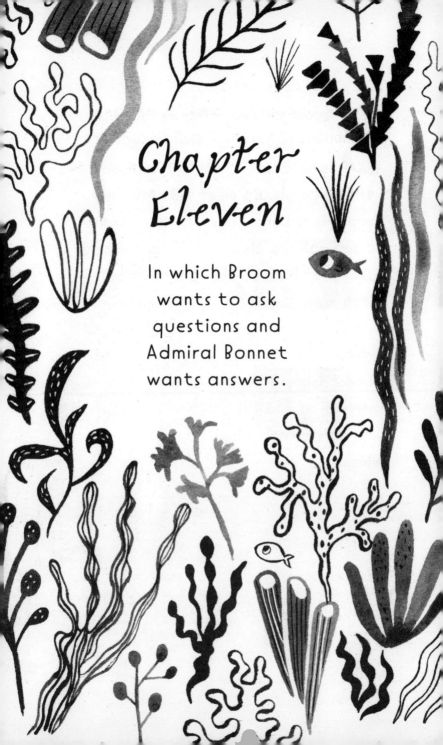

Chapter Eleven

In which Broom
wants to ask
questions and
Admiral Bonnet
wants answers.

*B*room phoned Admiral Bonnet.

'I know what the something is,' said Broom. 'She's a someone and I think you should meet her. Ms Tilly Topple is a Long Legs who has shrunk herself. She is also a witch in training.'

Admiral Bonnet didn't know what a witch was.

'I don't know either,' said Broom.

'Does she by any chance know the School Ghost?' asked Admiral Bonnet.

'Hold on and I'll ask her,' said Broom, who didn't know about the School Ghost himself.

'Ms Topple, do you by chance know the School Ghost?'

'I do,' said Tilly Topple. 'He lives in our school. Is he all right?'

'She does. And she wants to know if he's all right,' said Broom to Admiral Bonnet.

'He spent the night at Spokes',' said Admiral Bonnet. 'Spokes tells me he and the School Ghost are busy working on a surprise. What with a witch in training and a school ghost, surprises are turning up willy-nilly. I suggest we all meet at the café at gleetime.'

'Good plan,' said Broom.
With that settled, Broom
got back to his usual routine.
He touched his toes
fifty times. He
brushed his green fur, he
brushed his teeth and he
brushed his tootsies to
make sure they were clean.
The rain had stopped; Ms
Tilly Topple waited
outside in the sun on
an upturned plant pot.
Skittle, Brew and Pinch
were keen to see Ms
Tilly Topple for
themselves.
They soon came
hop-skipping
along.

'Hello,' said Skittle. 'Are you Ms Topple?'

'I am,' she said. 'But, please, call me Tilly.'

'I'm Skittle, this is Brew, and Pinch is my furry purry pet.'

'Hello, Tilly,' said Pinch.

'You have the longest tail I've ever seen,' said Tilly.

'And you have the most pointedest pointy hat I've ever seen,' said Pinch.

'It's our uniform at the witches' school,' said Tilly. 'I'm studying to be a witch.'

'How did you get here?' asked Brew.

'In a puff of pink smoke,' said Tilly.

'Wow!' said Skittle, Brew and Pinch together, but before they could ask her what a witch is, the greenhouse door opened and out came Broom, his hat on his head and his scarf round his neck. He was looking rather smart.

'This is Ms Tilly Topple,' said Broom.

'We know,' said Pinch.

'Oh. Well, I thought I'd show her Rubbish Island.'

'She came in a puff of pink smoke and she's studying to be a witch,' said Skittle.

And that's a fact actually,' added Pinch.

'I haven't got round to my list of questions,' said Broom. 'I thought I'd ask as we went along.'

'We'll come too,' said Skittle.

'Would you mind if I took a photo or two?' asked Tilly. She took out a small squarish thing and clicked it at the greenhouse, then at Pinch.

'It's a strange thing to do,' said Brew quietly to Skittle. 'Perhaps she's feeling nervous and the clicking makes her feel better.'

Broom placed tiny Tilly on his shoulder and they set off. But every time Broom was about to ask a question, Tilly would say, 'What's that?'

'What's that?' she said when she saw Bottle Mountain.

'That's the plastic bottles we fish out of the sea,' said Skittle. 'They have *Still* and *Sparkling* written on them. Now we know the words mean water.'

'It's a very large mountain,' said Tilly.

'That's nothing to how large it once was,' said Brew.

'Where do you come from, Tilly?' Broom asked his first question quickly but Tilly

said, 'What's down there?' and clicked
another photo.

'That's Turtle Bay. We'll go that way
through the Roo-Roo Woods,' said Broom.

He tried to ask his first question again
but Tilly said, 'Smile everyone,' and
click-click-click, she'd taken photos of
Skittle, Brew and Pinch in the Roo-Roo
Woods. She'd even stretched out her
arm and taken several photos of herself
sitting on Broom's shoulder.

It wasn't until they reached the
café, where Admiral Bonnet,
Captain Spoons, Hitch Stitch,
Barnacle Bow, Mug, Jug and
Baby Cup were waiting
with Ethel B Dina and
Granny Gull, that
Ms Topple had to
stop clicking

and face the many questions that needed answering.

'Would you like to see the photos I've taken?' she asked Admiral Bonnet.

'I would like answers,' said Admiral Bonnet firmly. 'First, what are you doing here? You're a Little Long Legs. And second, how did you get here?'

'I'm a witch in training,' said Tilly Topple, 'and to pass my Second Grade Spell exam I had to take myself to a place no witch has ever been. But I accidentally shrank myself and next thing I knew the School Ghost and I were here. I don't know how to get back. And if I don't get back soon I will miss Halloween.'

'Just a moment,' said Broom, asking a question not on his list. 'What actually is a witch?'

'A person with magic powers,' said Tilly. 'I'm a good witch and I use my powers to help people. So, to pass my Second Grade Spell exam I was putting a spell on your pumpkins to make them grow big. I didn't mean to frighten you.'

Broom thought about this for a moment then said, 'Do you mean you were sprinkling Halloween on them?'

Tilly Topple laughed. 'Don't you know what Halloween is?' she asked.

Chapter Twelve

In which the Tindims begin to understand what Halloween is and Jug remembers some boxes in the library marked UNKNOWN.

Tilly Topple did her best to describe Halloween.

'Blow my tin hat into a trumpet!' said Captain Spoons. 'It's nearly as bad as finding out all the bottles on Bottle Mountain were once filled with water.'

Jug had been drinking a cup of glee but he paused. 'Of course,' he said. 'That's it.'

'That's what?' said Captain Spoons. 'I'm more baffled than I was before.'

'Come on, Barnacle Bow and you too,

Hitch Stitch,' said Jug.
'We're going to fetch some
boxes from the library.' The
library was next door to the Fish
Hospital, down a lot of stairs. 'I think
we may now have the answer to a lot of
unexplained rubbish.'

'Can we help?' asked Skittle.

'No,' said Jug. 'Won't be long.'

When they were gone, Tilly said
cheerfully, 'Are there any more Tindims?'

Captain Spoons wasn't best pleased
that a shrunken Little Long Legs, witch
or not, had come to Rubbish Island
without an invitation.

'Now listen here, young witch,' he said, 'this is quite a windy pickle. What I want to know is, what will you do if your spell wears off and you become full size again? That would be a disaster for us and the whole island would be in danger.'

'Shrink me a teabag!' said Brew.

'Oh, that's a terrible thought!' said Mug.

'It won't and I won't,' said Tilly Topple.

'How can you be sure?' asked Admiral Bonnet.

'Because I can't remember which way round the spell went, and if I can't remember that, I'm stuck.'

'What can I say to a witch in training who we didn't invite to the island?' said Captain Spoons.

Admiral Bonnet was thinking of something wise when Jug, Barnacle Bow and Hitch Stitch returned from the library with three huge boxes marked: *UNKNOWN*.

'This is only a small part of the collection,' said Jug. Before he opened the boxes he added, 'Skittle and Brew, you are not to look.'

'Why not?' said Skittle and Brew together.

'Because what's inside is scary. Scrunch me a teabag, and do as you're told,' said Jug and opened the boxes.

Pinch immediately poked his nose in and

ran back to **Skittle**, his fur on end.

'It's horrid,' he said. 'Best not seen by a Tindim. *And that's a fact, actually.*'

Tilly Topple peered into the boxes. They were filled to the brim with:

plastic ghosts

plastic bats

plastic masks

plastic hats

plastic pumpkins

bits of plastic bunting

'Where did you find all this?' asked Tilly Topple.

'Fished it out of the sea,' said Hitch Stitch. 'Our motto is: "Rubbish today is treasure tomorrow". But we haven't been able to use any of this. It's all too frightening for little Tindims.'

'These things are a part of Halloween,' said Tilly Topple. 'But they shouldn't have been thrown into the sea.'

'Do Little Long Legs know about them?' asked Jug.

'Oh, yes,' said Tilly Topple. 'They're for the children's Halloween parties and when they go trick or treating.'

'What's the trick?' asked Brew.

'Well, if the children knock on a neighbour's door and the neighbour doesn't give them a treat, they play a trick on them.'

'That's not nice,' said Pinch. '*And that's a fact*'

'But why can't the Little Long Legs do treat or treat?' asked Skittle.

It was a good question and it hung in the air unanswered.

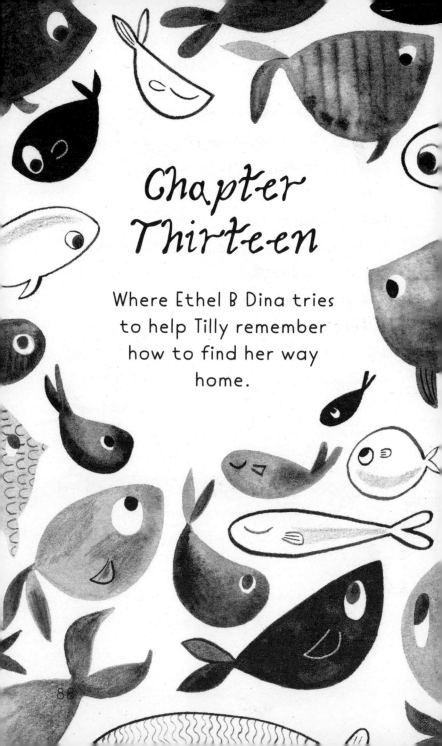

Chapter Thirteen

Where Ethel B Dina tries to help Tilly remember how to find her way home.

Tilly Topple had been on Rubbish Island nearly a week and Broom was enjoying having a guest in his greenhouse. It made a change to have someone to have glee with, someone to talk to about gardens and growing plants.

Tilly seemed very happy spending her time drawing Broom's plants and clicking at any Tindims she happened to meet. She was very good at asking questions.

She had many for Ethel B Dina. But when Ethel B Dina said, 'Do you think, my still and sparkling darling, that the School Ghost might remember the spell

you've forgotten?' Tilly had nothing
to say.

Ethel B Dina tried again. 'What were
you doing when you cast the spell?' she
asked.

'You mean the spell that brought me
here?'

'Yes, my still and sparkling darling
witch.'

Tilly thought for a moment and said, 'I
was wearing my invisible cloak. And the
School Ghost asked if he could come with
me. You see, none of the other witches
in training ever take him anywhere. We're

both teased — they call me Silly Tilly and they make fun of the School Ghost. Anyway, he climbed on to my broomstick behind me. I did feel silly when I said I wasn't sure if my spell would work. But next thing we knew — *whoosh* — we were here. My cloak was torn — a piece of it was missing — and my broomstick was gone.'

'Perhaps the broomstick is hiding,' suggested Skittle who, with Brew and Pinch, had been following Tilly wherever she went. They had been taking it in turns to wear her invisible cloak. You could see when Pinch had it on because his long tail stuck out from under it.

'What if the broomstick is hiding inside a piece of the invisible cloak?' said Brew. 'We wouldn't be able to see it, would we?'

'My still and sparkling darlings, of course, that's it. We must go and find Broom.'

It was Skittle's turn to wear the invisible cloak and only her legs and hands were visible.

'That's truly spooky,' said Broom, as Skittle took off the cloak and was visible again.

'We are here, my still and sparkling darling, to look for an invisible broomstick,' said Ethel B Dina.

'When you say broomstick, you don't mean a Broom like me?'

'No,' said Tilly. 'We mean a stick with twigs on the end.'

'Oh — a besom, a leaf-sweeper,' said

Broom, relieved. He didn't like the idea of there being another Broom, like himself but invisible, on the island.

'Well,' he said, 'the best way to find things that are lost is to think of the last place you were before you lost them.'

'I remember it was before I went to the pumpkin patch...' said Tilly Topple. 'Oh, yes, I was in the orchard.'

'Then it must be here, somewhere, *and that's a fact*,' said Pinch.

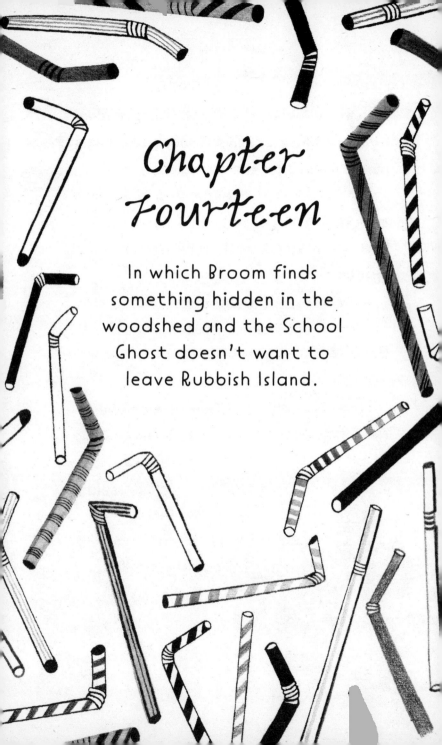

Chapter Fourteen

In which Broom finds something hidden in the woodshed and the School Ghost doesn't want to leave Rubbish Island.

Broom was a well-
organised gardener and
every log and stick he
picked up from the orchard
was stored in his woodshed.
'I've an idea where it might
be,' he said.

Ethel B Dina, Tilly
Topple, Skittle, Pinch and
Brew followed Broom to the
woodshed.

Broom stood them in a line and handed
them log after log and stick after
stick until the woodshed
was empty.

'Oh,' said Tilly,
disappointed.
'It's not there.'

Broom was beginning to understand that where there was nothing, something could well be hidden. He felt the four walls of the empty woodshed, and then he felt the floor.

'What about the corners?' said Pinch and suddenly Broom was holding something that no one could see until he pulled off the missing piece of the invisible cloak.

'My broomstick!' said Tilly Topple. 'How wonderful to have it back. Now all I need to do is remember the spell.'

That was something that Broom couldn't help with, but Ethel B Dina had an idea.

'Let's go and see what Spokes and the School Ghost are up to,' she said.

'No, no, no,' said the School Ghost when Ethel B Dina asked him if he remembered the spell Tilly had cast.

'I mean, yes, I do,' he said. 'But don't make me go back. I haven't had this much fun since 1723.'

'He's a brilliant mechanic,' said Spokes.

In the corner of Spokes' workshop was something large, covered in a cloth.

'What's that?' asked Brew.

'You tell them,' said Spokes to the School Ghost.

'It's a spooky secret surprise,' said the School Ghost.

Tilly lifted a corner of the cloth. 'Oooh,' she said. 'Could it get us home in time for Halloween?'

The School Ghost looked sad.

'Yes, it could. But I don't want to go home. Spokes listens to me — none of the witches do.'

'What if I told them how brilliant you are?' said Tilly Topple. 'And how you got us home for Halloween? You wouldn't want to miss that party, would you?'

'No!' said the School Ghost. 'But I don't want to

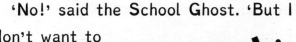

GO!'

He said **GO** so loudly that everyone put their hands over their ears.

'And I don't want you to go,' said Spokes. 'But you can't stay. This is Rubbish Island and we are Tindims. How about if you came to visit in the school holidays? If you remember the spell, that is.'

'You mean me?' said the School Ghost. 'That would be perfect. But what about Ms Tilly Topple?'

'Once has been wonderful,' said Tilly. 'The Tindims are right, though. A witch, even a shrunken witch in training, is a worry.'

Skittle put her arm round her and Broom said, 'As Pinch would say, *and that's a fact.* Actually, where is Pinch?'

At that moment they heard a terrible scream

and Pinch rushed out from under the cloth that covered the large spooky secret.

'That is the scariest something I've ever seen!' he said. 'What is it?'

Spokes looked proud. 'It's the spooky secret surprise.'

'Let's see it,' said Skittle and Pinch.

'It's still a secret,' said Spokes. 'We need one more neeptide to find the last piece and then it will be perfect.'

Chapter Fifteen

Where the School Ghost
gets a brand new name and
Tilly's cloak is mended.

*A*s no one knew what Spokes and the School Ghost were looking for, there was no way the other Tindims could help.

'It wouldn't be a secret or a surprise if you knew,' said Spokes.

Which was sort of true and sort of not true.

'But as we don't know what it is,' said Brew, 'how would finding the missing part on the shore spoil it?'

Which was a good point that Spokes took no notice of.

'That can happen when you can only think of one thing,' said Ethel B Dina wisely.

'What's that?' asked Brew.

'Oh, my still and sparkling darlings,' said Ethel B Dina, 'his mind is just on the spooky secret surprise.'

'Well, while we're waiting, the School Ghost should have a proper name,' said Skittle. 'School Ghost sounds...'

'Lost,' said Pinch. 'I would be lost if I was called the School Pet, and *that's a fact actually*.'

'As it happens,' Spokes said, 'my mind is on more than one thing. I've thought of a name for the School Ghost. Spooks. What do you think about that, School Ghost?'

'Spooks? I like it — and it goes so well with Spokes. Spokes and Spooks.'

'Perfect,' said Tilly.

Skittle, Pinch and Brew climbed up to the treehouse from where they could see Spokes on the beach with Spooks. Wherever Spokes went, Spooks followed. Spooks looked a bit more solid than he had before.

'I think if you don't have a name,
you could easily become invisible,' said
Skittle, 'and feel as if you're nothing.'

'Not even a something or a someone,'
said Brew.

'And that's not nice at all,' said Pinch.

Three more floodtides came and went
before Spokes found what he'd been
searching for. In the end, it was Spooks,
with his brand-new name, who found it.
Not on the beach, but in the library, and
with the help of Jug who had no idea why
it was useful.

Spokes was thrilled. 'The spooky secret
surprise will be ready to roll tomorrow,'
he announced.

This was good timing as Granny Gull had just finished mending Tilly Topple's invisible cloak. It had been a tricky job.

The Tindims were at the café for glee when Captain Spoons sighed and said, 'Something isn't right.'

Hitch Stitch agreed. 'We're not fishing the rubbish out of the sea, that's what's not right.'

'After all,' said Barnacle Bow, 'that's what we're supposed to be doing.'

'Hold that thought in a plastic bottle,' said Admiral Bonnet. 'We can't just let Spokes and Spooks present their spooky secret surprise and then *wish-bish* Ms Tilly Topple and Spooks are gone. This is a moment that needs to be marked.'

'A new celebration to add to our calendar,' said Ethel B Dina. 'Oh, my still and sparkling darlings — we can have **TINDIWEEN**!'

'What's that?' asked Pinch.

'A party. In other words — our Halloween. But without the scary bits.'

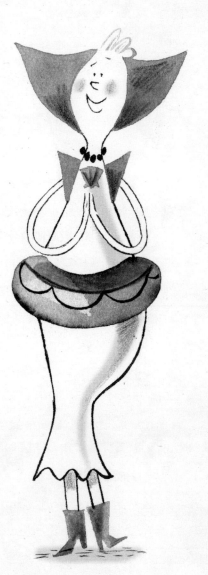

Chapter Sixteen

In which Ethel B Dina sings to Tilly and the Tindims make their costumes for Tindiween.

So much rubbish had washed up while they had been solving the mystery of Tilly Topple, Spooks and the pesky pumpkins that the Tindims decided the best thing that could be done with it was to make Tindiween costumes.

Mug was in charge, filling sacks with rubbish just as she had for the Brightsea Festival. She handed a sack to every Tindim. The Tindim who made the best costume with the least rubbish would win the competition. The prize was a big slice of Granny Gull's delicious pumpkin pie to take home.

Tilly asked if she could join in.

'Of course, you're one of us now,' said Barnacle Bow. 'When you've passed your exam,' he added quietly, 'would you encourage your Little Long Legs to make their own Halloween costumes? And Long Legs not to buy plastic party things.' He sang a Tindims ditty.

No plastic pumpkins long Legs please,
They aren't meant to float in seas

'I'll remember that,' said Tilly. 'First I must cast the spell that will take Spooks and me back to the school. The trouble is even Spooks can't remember the beginning or the end of the spell. I don't know if it will work unless I know which way round it goes.'

Ethel B Dina had an idea. 'When the
little fishes are stuck in plastic bottles,
I sing to them and then they are free.
Quite how it works I don't know, but
perhaps one of my songs might untangle
your memory.'

'It's worth a try,' said Tilly and
followed Ethel B Dina to her flat in the
Fish Hospital.

Pinch, Skittle and Brew
went to hide and Pinch
wrapped his tail round his
ears eight times.

Tilly lay on a sofa in
Ethel B Dina's sitting
room.

'Ready?' said Ethel B Dina
and began to sing.

It was a terrible sound.

'Oh,' said Tilly, 'it's come back to me
... it goes...'

'Frolicking fish! Don't say it aloud,'
said Ethel B Dina. 'You should be over
the sea before the first word of the spell
is uttered. And ideally hanging in mid-
air. We don't want you growing big while
you're on Rubbish Island. Think what
could happen — you might topple the
whole island into the sea. That would be

a disaster that no amount of my singing
could put right.'

No one knew how it was possible
for Ethel B Dina's song to make Tilly
remember her spell. Though Skittle did
wonder if Spokes' and Spooks' spooky
secret surprise might have something to
do with it.

Chapter Seventeen

In which the Tindiween
party is a great success
and all is ready for
Spokes' and Spooks'
spooky secret surprise.

The day of Tindiween, everyone was busy making their spooky costumes and by the time the moon had risen they were ready. The scooped-out pumpkins had twinkling candles in them and Ethel B Dina had hung them round the café.

The Tindims arrived, one after another, each giving the other a fright until they all found it so funny that they burst out laughing.

Granny Gull had made the biggest pumpkin pie ever. It sat in the middle of the long table, smiley and pleased with itself and looking mouth-wateringly delicious. All along the table were bottles of Broom's Roo-Roo pop and Granny Gull's Roo-Roo jelly.

Everyone was having so much fun, they'd nearly forgotten about Spokes' and Spooks' spooky secret surprise. Then there was a noise, as if some huge

contraption was puffing and wheezing towards them.

'What's that?' asked Admiral Bonnet.

They saw a wheel with lights on it. It was spinning round and round but how it came to be floating off the ground no one had the foggiest idea.

'I think that's the spooky secret surprise,' said Captain Spoons, looking through his telescope.

The wheel came closer and closer and stopped outside the café.

'What is it?' Brew asked Spokes who was sitting on a bicycle saddle, turning the pedals.

Spooks was floating around, full of excitement. 'It's a contraption to help fish bottles out of the sea,' he said.

'Or it was,' said Spokes. 'We've changed it so it can take Tilly and Spooks right out over the sea. Tilly can cast her spell and
wish-bish-whoosh,
she and Spooks will be back at the school for trainee witches. But first we have a show to perform.'

The machine lit up, music played and Tilly Topple began to sing. She had the sweetest voice and with Spooks on backing vocals they sang many songs.

Tilly ended with this:

'Where is the good in goodbye?
It's the hardest of things to say.
Where is the hell in hello,
When hello is the start of a day?
Where is the fair in farewell?
For it seems quite unfair to us.
And as all the words can tell,
Goodbye is terrible fuss.'

While Spooks sang:

'Doo-**boo**-**boo**-**bhop**-**hoo**

Shoo-doo-doo-**booohoo**.'

Ethel B Dina joined in the last verse with Tilly.

'Goodbye is just a reason for hello,
Farewell, we will see you again.
Tindims will always be here
    Come sun, or snow or rain.'

And Spooks sang:

Doo-**boo**-boo-**bhop**-hoo
Shoo-doo-doo-**booo**hoo.'

Chapter Eighteen

Where no one wants the party to end and no one likes goodbyes.

*O*nly when the
show was over
did the Tindims
have a better look
at what Spooks and Spokes had made.
It was a handsome machine built from a
wooden cartwheel held together with bits
of wood and rope.

'You see,' said Spokes, shining a
pumpkin lamp to where Tilly's broomstick
was in place, 'that's where you sit, Tilly.'

Broom, being tall, lifted her up. 'Have you got your invisible cloak?' he asked as Spooks sat behind her.

'Yes, it's here,' said Tilly. 'Oh dear, I'm not good at goodbyes.'

'Neither am I,' said Broom with a tear in his eye.

Spokes took his seat that worked the wheel and slowly the arm of the machine extended like a crane,

taking Tilly Topple and Spooks over
the sea.

The arm was long and heavy and for
a terrible moment it looked as if Spokes
and his spooky secret surprise were about
to tumble with Tilly and Spooks into the
ocean.

'The button,' shouted Spooks and just
in time Spokes pressed the release button
and the long arm zoomed neatly back in
on itself.

'Now, my still and sparkling darling,'
called Ethel B Dina, 'the spell, the spell!'

Over the sea there was a burst of
sparks and a puff of pink smoke. Then
nothing.

'Let's hope Tilly and Spooks made it
home,' said Skittle.

'We may never know,' said Brew.

And for once Pinch didn't say, 'And
that's a fact,' for the fact was that
nobody knew one way or the other.

Chapter Nineteen

A small footnote.

Time passed, two hopeseas, which is what the Tindims call spring, had blossomed and Broom was in his garden when a package attached to seven red balloons floated down to him. He opened it. Inside was a letter from Tilly Topple and another for Spokes from Spooks. But what took Broom's breath away were the photos and drawings that Tilly had sent. Broom rushed to the café to ask Ethel B Dina to read Tilly's letter to him.

134

Dear Broom,

Thanks to all your help, I won the First Class prize for my work on the Tindims of Rubbish Island.

Last term I became a teacher. My class and I made our own Halloween costumes. I took your clever Tindim idea and gave each member of my class a sack full of odds and bobs and they had to make a spooky secret surprise without using ANY plastic. It was a huge success.

Spooks is his old self again. He is counting the days until he can waft to Rubbish Island and see his best friend, Spokes.

Thank you for having me, I so loved your island. I think of it often and of all you dear Tindims. I hope you like the pictures.

Love, Tilly

There were photos of each of the Tindims and drawings as well.

'You know what this means,' Spokes said to Broom when he saw the pictures.

'Yes. Nothing can sometimes be more than something and might even be someone special.'

'It means,' said Spokes, 'we'll have to build an art gallery for the pictures.'

And they both laughed and laughed until their tummies jelly-jiggled.

'What's an art gallery?' said Broom.

The End

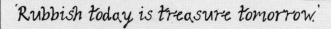

'Rubbish today is treasure tomorrow.'

HANGING BATS AND GHOSTS

BATS: Use a cereal box to cut out wings and triangles for ears.

Use a plastic bottle or tin for the body, but make sure the wings/ears fit. Ask a Long Legs to make a hole in the bottle/tin and thread string through it to hang your bat.

Paint the bottle/tin, or cover it in black fabric, add the cardboard wings and ears and let your bat swoop.

GHOSTS: use a bottle cap for the head. Ask a Long Legs to make a hole in the top for string to go through. Hang white fabric or a plastic bag cut jaggedly over the cap. Give your ghost a painted face. Whhhhoooo! It's ready to fly with the bats.

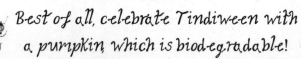

Best of all, celebrate Tindiween with a pumpkin, which is biodegradable!